BACK IN MY DAY

Evelyn's 1920's

LAUREN WAITE
& EMILY BRUCE

 FriesenPress

One Printers Way
Altona, MB R0G 0B0
Canada

www.friesenpress.com

ISBN
978-1-03-912190-4 (Hardcover)
978-1-03-912189-8 (Paperback)
978-1-03-912191-1 (eBook)

1. JUVENILE FICTION, HISTORICAL

Distributed to the trade by The Ingram Book Company

To our boys Benjamin and Braxton;
May you learn to love, and love to learn.

Hello! My name is Evelyn.
I am **ninety-five**.
Many things have happened
in the time I've been **alive**.
I could go on forever,
but I'll focus on a **few**.
Let me share my stories and
I'll teach you something **new**.

So come along with me, my friend. I'll take you on a ride. Let's explore the **1920s**, and I will be your guide.

It was a time for MUSiC, catchy tunes with great pizzazz, A brand-new kind of sound, and the name for it was jazz.

The music brought new dances,
and boy did we have fun!
A **Foxtrot** or the **Shimmy**,
and of course the **Charleston**.

On Friday nights Mom dressed up in her silver **flapper dress**.
She wore a matching headband and Dad always looked his **best**.

What about the toys, you ask?
So many I could share . . .
Tinkertoys and pedal cars
and the teddy bear.

There were **Tiddlywinks** and **yo-yos** and circus toys too,
Raggedy Ann and **crayons**,
just to name a few.

The **prices** sure were different down at the **corner store**.
A dozen **eggs** were thirty cents and **Milk** was thirty-four.

For only one dollar you could
go and see a **show**,
And for five little cents,
grab an **ice cream cone** to go.

Before the 1920s,
only some people had cars.
They were for the rich and famous
and for those movie stars.

And then before you knew it,
there were cars both **left** and **right**,
So somebody invented a brand-new
traffic light!

It had three coloured lights that would guide you on your way, **Yellow**, **green**, and **red**, just like the lights we have today.

Back in my day things were different.
So much has changed since then.
It's been so fun to be your guide and live it all again.
I've loved our time together,
but it's time for me to go.
There's so much more to share and
so much for you to know.
Known as the roaring twenties,
they were anything but boring!
I hope you'll take some time to do your own exploring.

Love Evelyn

1928

Steamboat Willie

For your own exploring!

The first bulldozer

"KING OF JAZZ"

LOUIS ARMSTRONG

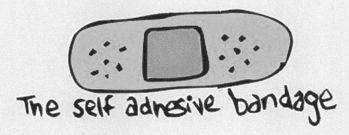

The self adhesive bandage

N°5

COCO CHANEL

1924

THE FIRST Winter Olympics

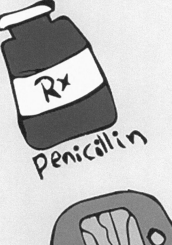

Rx

Penicillin

RISE OF RADIO

BABE RUTH

The electric blender